Before and after WW [...] until he branched out o[...] drove a six-wheeled truck up and down the UK motorways.

He has a son who is a builder in Durham, and a daughter who lives close by.

RJB's claim to fame since graduating to a civilian, a London-based firm used his premises as the location for a film. RJB's hand did appear inadvertently in a shot, but unfortunately it was unrecognizable. This film has been shown worldwide including the BBC. The credits include: 'Pyrotechnics by R J Blackmore'.

Basil

09-10

R J Blackmore

My boots and my kitbag in my luxurious accommodation (lower right).

Date: mid-1943
Location: Eritrea

Illumination supplied by a 10-ton Fiat lorry that we had nicked from the Italian army. This vehicle was ran continuously midday to midnight, it had to to supply power for a radiogram to play our single record continuously.

RJB, one of the now dwindling band of 39rs, was called up with the rest of the TA and refused to take exemption on farm work and instead spent the first two years of WWII at Coast Defence, Kent. Then on 11 June 1942, he had his 21st Birthday aboard QE2, bound for a secret destination, and embarked at Genifia onto a sandy beach of unbelievable depth and width and then later on to Egypt.

Then followed another tour down the Nile and stopped just outside Khartoum in time to eat a Christmas dinner of tinned chicken in a tent on the sand. The temperature was between 100 and 120 degrees. He toured Sudan and Eritrea until late 1945 and then another leisurely stroll up the coast to Benghazi and sat the war out until 1946.

School photo from about 1930 shows RJB front row, third from left.

Rockness

R. J. Blackmore

Published 2010 by arima publishing

www.arimapublishing.com

ISBN 978 1 84549 417 9

© R. J. Blackmore 2010

All rights reserved

This book is copyright. Subject to statutory exception and to
provisions of relevant collective licensing agreements, no part of this
publication may be reproduced, stored in a retrieval system, or
transmitted in any form or by any means, without the prior written
permission of the author.

Printed and bound in the United Kingdom

Typeset in Garamond 12/16

This book is sold subject to the conditions that it shall not, by way
of trade or otherwise, be lent, re-sold, hired out, or otherwise
circulated without the publisher's prior consent in any form of
binding or cover other than that which it is published and without a
similar condition including this condition being imposed on the
subsequent purchaser.

In this work of fiction, the characters, places and events are either
the product of the author's imagination or they are used entirely
fictitiously. Any resemblance to actual persons, living or dead, is
purely coincidental.

Swirl is an imprint of arima publishing.

arima publishing
ASK House, Northgate Avenue
Bury St Edmunds, Suffolk IP32 6BB
t: (+44) 01284 700321
www.arimapublishing.com

Contents

Preface

Rockness has been conjured up by an old codger who goes back to the times when this yarn is set he can well remember most except perhaps the sweep children, although the chimney sweep and donkey cart is well remembered. Although he may look it RJB is not a centurion yet but is looking forward to a letter from Buckingham Palace, he has spent many a long hour plodding along behind a shire horse.

The chapter Reverend Holly is folklore as told by his old Mum, go on you've read so far, be a devil buy a copy of the book, buy a copy for each of your siblings and let them read Rev. Holly, it's not blasphemous, go on read and be happy.

This was his finest hour

Introduction
Rockness Hall

Repairs and renovations had been made to the hall in readiness for the new owner to arrive on 29th September bringing with him all the portable equipment from his farming estate in Yorkshire. The train duly arrived at daybreak to be unclouded in reverse order to being loaded, live stock, then farm staff furniture and effects, furniture for the hall.

The trucks containing bulky farm machinery shunted into the station sidings and brought forward to the unloading bays as required.

Everything cleared before the end of the week when payments would be due.

Some of the harsh life of the underlings on an exposed area of Norfolk.

A hint of the poaching necessary to provide sustain from small earnings.

Chapter 1
Toing and Froing

Toing and Froing

Froing and Toing

Rumour and counter rumour

At last it was confirmed, Rockness Hall been sold.

Standing empty for years, paint peeling from its many windows and doors, shabby and unkempt, it had taken a large gang of workmen to restore it to its former splendour.

Wooden scaffolding had grown around its many angled walls, ladders and workmen ascending and descending like pieces of a giant complicated game, pails being pulled up and lowered on rope pulleys, as a cobweb, at the centre of which controlling its many meshes the foreman, Willie Moore, black jacket and bowler hatted, always a sheaf of papers in hand, constantly on the move, inspecting for lax workmanship, perfection the new owner required, and very near perfection he would get.

In the great dining hall the foreman stood quietly watching the master craftsman carving oak panelling to match and repair a frieze that circled the room, leaving as quietly as he had entered not to break the carver's concentration, to emerge from a roof window seconds later to check that each roofing slate was trimmed and matched exactly.

At one o-clock a whistle blew, men appeared from all corners of the house to sit around the walls of the back court yard, overcoats as cushions, wicker baskets or string bags containing their meagre food.

Sitting in groups according to their trade, the master craftsmen of each group easily recognised, he alone wore a bowler hat, the rest cloth caps.

A man in the group of carpenters spoke, voice muffled and indistinct through a mouthful of bread and cheese.

"Yew see he when he come round?"

"Yer mean Wex the new owner?"

"Ah."

"Whoi?"

"Oi see he, he say that there winder Oi juss made and put in the big bedroom wore too loose, it'll rattle he say, say it'll rattle in the wind, Yer know wott he went an done?"

A small spray of bread crumbs from his mouth as the man next to him mumbled through cheeks stuffed with food.

"He took his shut knife out o his trousers pocket an hacked grut lumps orf on ut, not only do Oi gotter make annover, Oi carn not use thisun on no other job."

"Sarve yer right bor, yew orter made ut right fust toime."

"Wore aright, iffun owd Bill Smiff hada daubed a mite o paint ont, ud still be there."

Five thirty, the whistle blew, shovels and trowels were washed, saws a wipe with an oily rag, no one dare put a tool away before knocking off time.

A few men who lived within a radius of four or five miles set off to walk home, the rest lived rough in the out buildings, straw to sleep on, a sack or overcoat to keep out the cold.

"Wot yer got in that there pot bor?"

There had been a general drift into the area of the harness room where a fire was soon lit, the speaker, a tall man in a paint-splattered coat, a cap rather too large for him resting on his ears, causing the top part of each ear to stand out at right angles to his head.

"Mite o rabbit an a few taters thas all."

"Looks enough fer two!"

"My owd woman made ut fer har husban, far as Oi know she only got one an he wan ut, wot yer got?"

"Bread an cheese ony Oi ete all the cheese yesterday, how yer gonna cook that there?"

"Tis cooked my owd woman say Oi gotta star ut every couple o minutes."

He stood watching his cast-iron pot on the fire, watch on the end of its chain in one hand, wooden spoon in the other, every two minutes the spoon was dipped in the pot of stew, turned a complete circle and withdrawn. It was woman's work to cook, most of the older men preferring to eat cold food than be seen heating food on the fire.

Heated to his satisfaction a stick was inserted in the handle of the stew pot and lifted from the fire, when standing the cook was six feet six inches tall, very thin, a large bushy moustache that covered his mouth.

There was no table, a wooden bench lined the walls, the pot was placed on the floor, he sat, legs straddled over it, he removed his cap hand inside it he wiped his face, a few strands of hair, sweat plastered to his bald head. Bent double head between his knees he ate, a wooden spoon full of the mixture aimed into his mouth, the over flow some returning to the pot, some onto floor and legs, the rabbit bones sucked and slurped clean were spat toward the fire, now occupied by another amateur cook. The solid part of the stew eaten, without straightening his back a hand fumbled around a jacket pocket and withdrew a thick slice of bread, broken and pushed into the gravy, it too was splattered into his mouth. The meal over he straightened his back, with his right forefinger slightly bent, swept the right side of his moustache into his mouth where it was sucked clean, the operation was then repeated on the left side of his face, both fingers wiped simultaneously on his jacket, his meal was over.

Jed Farr the master plasterer entered, and watched for a while a small timid man heating his pot on the fire. Jed six feet of brawn and muscle, under his bowler a face that had seen no razor since his first attempt at removing boyish fuzz, when a gashed ear caused him to vow never to shave again.

"How be me Wilf?"

"Not a mucher Jed, this bloody smoke Oi carn see ma wittles be they done or be they not."

"Not a man's wuk acookun Wilf, why doan e bring the missus down, she could earn a bit o money, we'd pay she ter cook our mite o grub."

"Oi might if ut were wuff me while."

"Yar muvver ould look arter the kids ount she?"

"Ah she might at that do Oi gie she a bob er two."

"How many younguns yew got now bor?"

"About nine Oi reckon."

"The oldest, doan yew call she Daisy."

"Bring she down anal, Oi loik the look o she."

Monday morning the spring wagonette that brought the workers in from their home town of Stocton some ten miles away, always full of men now crowded, with Wilf's wife, Em, their daughter Daisy, their belongings, a bundle of rags and coats as their bedding, and a sack containing food and cooking utensils.

During midday dinner break, several men brought into the scullery where Wilf had installed Em, iron pots to be heated ready for knocking off time. Em had followed one of the men up the steep wooden stairway, and returned three minutes later and placed a shilling on the table, Wilf sat on a box by the fire, sucking an empty clay pipe without moving. No specific contract was made for cooking, if vegetables needed peeling a few would be placed aside for Wilf and Em, or a few coppers payable at the end of the week.

Five-thirty the men called for their pots, hot handles wrapped in cap or apron tail, the fire place empty, Jed entered.

"Wotcher Wilf."

"Wotcher Jed - Daisy toime yer were abed."

"But father tain't late yit."

"Goo."

Daisy reluctantly climbed out of sight up he steep stairs, Jed put a sixpence on the table and followed.

"Father father" was screamed from upstairs, then silence.

Wilf still sat sucking his empty pipe, staring into the fire,.

Heavy hobnailed boots clomped along the upstairs passage and down the stairs.

"Yew never tole Oi Oi were the fust."

With that Jed placed another sixpence on the table.

Chapter 2
The Sweep

Everything about him appeared black, from his tall silk hat, his black kerchief, frock coat, trousers and boots, the only nearly white parts were the whites of his eyes, even the grey parts of his beard tinged with soot. His donkey pattered it's way up the drive, iron shod wheels of the small wagon crunching on the gravel. By the back kitchen door the sweep unharnessed the donkey and tethered it to graze on a patch of unkempt grass. Two small black bundles of rags moved and materialised into a very small girl and an even smaller boy, who threw out of the wagon bundles of black sacking which they carried indoors.

The sweep emerged from the front door and walked sedately to the centre of the front lawn where he stood, watch in hand gazing up at the chimneys to be joined by the foreman.

"Morning Mr Sweep."

"Morning Mr Moore."

"Tis a grand day!"

"We need dry weather, the soot doesn't cling so much."

"They're working?"

"They're both, the girl should be out in

The sweep consulted his watch,

"In about one minute, any quicker, she's not doing her job proper, much slower and she's slacking, the boy will be longer, he doesn't know the job yet."

"They won't get stuck?"

"Here never, the best sweep's chimneys for many a mile, got toe bricks to."

"Toe bricks!, never heard of them in my part of the country."

"Some brickies but them in, a brick across the corner every fourth course as good as a ladder."

A hand appeared from a chimney top, another holding a short handled hoe, a head, hair matted with soot, shoulders, with both hands on the chimney top, a heave then a small naked girl sat on the coping bricks, turning to face those on the lawn it was obvious that she was approaching womanhood, naked scratched blackened breasts outlined against the sky.

"She's growing up Mr Sweep."

"Tis a pity, tis a pity, one of the best I've had, bought her for half a guinea."

"You bought her?"

"From a man in a pub, don't know where he came from,

you've seen the sort, a long tale of woe, wife too ill to work, kids ill, gave him half a guinea, and half a gallon of gin."

"What will you do with her when she's too big for the chimneys?"

"Tis a problem, tis a problem, may let her out to an inn or a bawdy house, she's strong could earn good money. May bring her into the house, my wife's been dead these three years, God rest her soul, tis cold the bed with no woman."

"Do they ever get stuck up a chimney?"

"Tis a problem that's why I work 'em in twos, one stuck, the other follows up, and can usually push or pull 'em free, if not a bit of rope round the ankles often does the trick, or a rope dropped from the top for them to pull on. It's surprising though how a bit of smoke from a smudge fire shifts some of 'em. It's only a last resort we have to take a few bricks out, some of the bends are a bit tricky for them as don't know the best way to get up. If we do take bricks out we only put them back with sand and water, makes it easier next time. We don't often lose one, occasionally a smudge fire is left on to long, it's a bad business to have to take a dead-un out, it upsets the others for a while."

A second head appeared from an adjacent chimney, face, hair, body, black with soot, open sores on elbows and knees that were not yet hardened by use.

The sweep waved his arm, bodies shoulders, head then arms disappeared from view, ten more blocks of chimneys, towering high and ornate, four chimneys to a block to be climbed and cleaned by small arms and legs.

The foreman remained on the lawn, eyes on the chimneys where whisps of soot indicated the children were still working, he was rejoined by the sweep.

"Small the children are Mr Sweep!"

"Tis true, tis true, much food only makes them big too quick, girls I find last longer than boys."

"That girl up there!"

Moore pointed to where puffs of soot from a fresh chimney showed where a child was working energetically near the top.

"That girl, I would give her a roof over her head, I'm a widower, five sovereigns I have in my pocket this day."

"We can talk Mr Moore, we can talk."

Chapter 3
Train

Mr Wex, a widower, the new owner of Rockness Hall, had inherited from his grandfather a large fortune, which, added to his own not inconsiderable wealth had enabled him to sell his farm in the north of England and purchase, on the coast of Norfolk, Rockness Hall, included in the estate, the adjacent farms and most of the dwellings and trade establishments in Rockness village.

He was bringing from Yorkshire by special train his furniture and personal effects, most of the household servants and staff, the farm workers, their families and furniture. All the paraphernalia of a large farm, horses carts, wagons implements, cows calves, pigs a large flock of sheep. All had been loaded onto the train in their predetermined order, the last to be loaded a stable of percheron horses, to the untrained eye each indistinguishable from the next, except the pair of stud stallions who stood head and shoulders above their harem of mares.

Loading the train had taken many days, but had been

completed on schedule by dusk on the 28th of September, the train to travel overnight, due to arrive at Hotchly station first light on Michaelmass day.

A holiday atmosphere had grown over Rockness Hall and the village, as wagons had been prepared to help fetch the train load from the station, wagon wheels had been removed, the iron axles lubricated with evil smelling grease that had been made from boiling dead animals, scratches on paint work painted over, many evenings spent polishing harness brasses, the women mended patched garments to be worn for the great occasion. The hob-iron had been borrowed back and forth as boots were repaired and hob nails replaced.

All the Rockness men, women and children who were fit enough, went to the station on the 28th ready to make an early start with the unloading next day. Bundles of straw had been placed into empty railway box vans to sleep on. As evening wore on, fires were lit, bread toasted, strips of fat bacon held on green sticks over the flames, sizzled as salty fat dripped onto the fire. Cast iron kettles steamed with rattling lids as water was boiled for tea making.

Bottles of home made beer and wine made frequent rounds. First one group then another, led spontaneous community singing, the songs ranging from hymns and carols to folk songs, political ditties to bawdy rude songs.

Couples slipped way into the darkness, returning flushed and disheveled. At last the excited children who had been playing tag and hide-seek around the quieter parts of the sidings were rounded up. Who was to sleep where and with whom was agreed on. Beds made with an assortment of blankets many made from scraps of wool gleaned from hedgerows or fences. Some slept fully clothed, with legs inside corn sacks, at long last, after a few good natured grumbles, the odd child snivelling, a few subdued giggles the camp slept.

Early next morning, the horsemen were first to stir from their temporary lodgings, heavy hobnailed boots clomping along concrete paths as they fed and watered horses and rekindled fires.

In the quietness of the sleeping town a church clock struck five times, a train whistled in the distance, signal control wires clattered, signal arms clanked into position, with a cushing of steam, and a clanking of steel wheels over rail joints, the train pulled into the station, the station was awake.

Standing apart from the farm hands the porters had awaited the arrival of the special train, one swinging from side to side a signal lamp, green side toward the engine, ever slower the train approached, when the cattle trucks were opposite the cattle pens the light was turned to red, steam hissed, metal to metal brakes screeched, with scarcely a jolt the engine came to rest opposite the porters.

The porters moved nearer the engine to talk to the engine crew.

"Lo Arfur bor."

"Lo Ted."

"Good run Arfur bor?"

"Ah nosser bad."

"Wot yar passengers loike bor?"

"Awright Oi spect, they down half tolk funny, Oi doan know wot they be on about half the toime."

The fireman silent till now chipped in.

"Yew did when we got that there red signal."

The porters sensing a good story leaned on the engine and gazed upwards.

"Whoi teellus wot happened bor."

"Us got this here red bout ha'parss free, as Oi pulled up the owd gals scrambled down ont track and lifted their skuts, they were awl busy so Oi lugged open the owd steam regulator, the owd ingun she shot sparks up int air higher nor yew could see, the wheels skiddeded, yew should a seed they owd gals run, us knew wot they were on about then."

"Yew allus were a rotten pair o'buggers."

"Ah, dew tew git they cattle orf, us gotter take they empty cattle trucks back ter Cambridge ready for market cum Monday, doan yew slip about us'll be here cum Monday."

Kettle lids and tin mugs rattled as tea was made and offered to the occupants of the train, children ran back and forth along the length of the train vying to be the first to discover the contents of each truck. The train load itself now awake with a medley of sound, cows separated from calves bawled with anxiety, calves answering in a higher tone. Hungry young piglets squealed as they fought for a place at the sow's udder. "Horses whinnied, those in the trucks stamping on the wooden floor as they impatiently fretted to be freed.

Overall blanketing many small sounds, a continuous baaing from the truck loads of sheep. The sheep being the slowest walkers were unloaded first, as the doors were opened, the sheep dogs leaped along the backs of the sheep, snarling and snapping, encouraging them to join those already unloaded. When on the road the shepherd led the way, resplendent in his best smock, by it's embroidered design easily recognisable as not being of local origin, his floppy Tam-O-Shanter type hat of homespun wool covering his ears almost to his eyes. As he walked in front of the flock he gave an occasional trilling whistle, to which all the sheep responded with a chorus of loud baa's. They marched, the bell sheep close behind the shepherd her bell giving a constant tinkle, a couple of girls walked each side to shut gates and guide back wanderers, the shepherds boy trailed behind with his cart to pick up lame stragglers.

The cows unloaded, those with calves let loose in pens to suckle, the dairy cows tied to a fence to be milked by hand.   Buckets and three legged stools were produced, Charlie, the head cow-man called for volunteers from the unknown train party, milking time was in session.

Charlie lifted his head from the cow he was milking.

"Dew any buddy want any they can come and git ut, ut ownt keep arter be'en shook up awl night."

Many of those not milking fetched cans or jugs, squatting opposite the milker to catch their container full. Head pressed tightly into the flank of the cow, the milker with a flick of the wrist could accurately direct a jet of milk many yards, the usual target to get milk as high as possible under the girls' skirts.

Charlie had finished milking a cow and was filling a variety of containers from his bucket, nearby one of his men was on his knees in front of a woman from the train.

"Wot yew think yew adowan there?"

"Oi ony a-wippun milk from this here gals leg."

"Dew yew git on a -milkun, Iffun anyun's gowan ter

woip milk orfun har leg ut's agowan ter be me."

Chapter 4
House Parade

Mr Wex spread the word that everyone was to be on the front lawn at six o'clock next morning as he wished to speak to them,

From five thirty onwards small groups of people began to appear near the lawn, the entrances were soon blocked as no one wished to be near the front. As the grand-father clock in the hallway struck six Mr Wex opened the front door, the first sight many had seen of him. Tall straight as a ram-rod, eyes fierce below bushy black eye-brows, riding whip in hand, his posture, the way he wore his clothes, all indicated many years service as an officer in a crack cavalry regiment. At the top of the steps he halted, glared round at the various groups, then roared.

"I want everyone at the foot of the steps."

Hurrying, jostling, pushing forward, at last quiet, again came the thunderous voice.

"Is everyone here?"

No one dare answer.

"Horse-keeper are all the stable party here?"

Tom the horse-keeper, now rheumatic and bent after many years working outside in all weathers at Rockness Hall.

"A Zur all hoss men be here."

"Are all the cow-men here?"

A fidgety silence, as if each member of the crowd hoped for someone else to answer.

Mr Wex, needle points of his immaculately waxed moustache quivering with indignation, again roared.

"Damn and blast, are all of the cow-men here?"

One of the youngest yard-boys timidly answered.

"Charlie ain't ere."

"Any who in gods name is Charlie?"

"Charlie's the cow-man an he ain't here."

"Fetch him boy if he's not here in two minutes, him and you are sacked."

He continued to address the crowd.

"Are all the regular day-men here?"

A murmur of assent, the dairy-maids, the house-hold staff were all present when the boy returned with a message.

"Charlie say he calven a cow an'carn come yit."

Met with a torrent of speech from the top of the steps.

"Damn and blast his hide he's sacked."

He continued his speech, he expected them to be

honest, or they'd be sacked, work hard or they'd be dismissed his service, he was still in full spate when he saw a figure overcoat and dinner bag over his shoulder, leaving the cattle yards.

"That man."

Charlie continued his steady plodding away from the yard.

"That man, that man leaving the cattle lines with his great coat over his shoulder, come here."

At the same pace, Charlie turned and walked the length of the lawn, the crowd parting to let him through.

"The devil take you, and who are you, that you can walk away from my parade with a face like a yard of bear's guts?"

Bellowed the now thoroughly irate Mr Wex.

"O'im Charlie Wayne, till a coupler minutes agoo Oi were cowman here, till Oi wore juss bin sacked."

"Why were you not on my parade?"

"Oi've bin up orl night a'calven one o' they cows an' coun'n leave she till now."

"By the great Lord Harry man, do you consider that more important than my parade?"

"Yezur."

"Any why in Hell's name should that be?"

"Iffen you loose all yar calves, you won't ha no cows and you ownt not want a cow-man."

"You were a military man?"

"Yezur."

"Regiment?"

"Second Lancers, Zur."

"Rank?"

"Farrier sargeant Zur."

"Why then a cow-man?"

"Oi wanted ter wuk here Zur, but there were a good hoss-man here."

"Get back to your cattle lines man."

"He roared even louder."

"But let no one else try that trick on, or you can be sure he will get his marching orders."

Charlie turned and walked slowly away.

"Sarjeant Wayne."

"Zur."

"You're promoted to fore-man, dismiss the parade."

Chapter 5
Harvest Festival

All day Friday and Saturday barrows and baskets were loaded with produce and taken to the church for the harvest festival; on Saturday, Mrs Jeeves the vicars wife, her daughter, and one or two of the selected church goers, used the pick of the produce to decorate the more important parts of the church including the vicarage pew.

The tenant farmers wives, and wives of the local tradesmen, decorated their own pews'. The back of the church and belfry were decorated by the village people after they had finished work on Saturday evening.

The church only partly lit by paraffin lamps, people busy in all parts, decorating with flowers and produce. Kneeling behind the lectern delicately threading flowers among leaves, was Jessie Jeeves, at thirty, still single tall, thin, lank black hair rat's tailed down from a blotchy white face, only a devout coward could call her anything but ugly. Nearly finished her work of art, she idly watched the scene through the fronds on the lectern.

Emmie the vicarage maid was very busy at the back of

the church, almost hidden by the vestry door, standing on the back of a pew, supported by two of the village boys, she was busily arranging large potatoes on a window sill.

As Jessie watched it seemed as if she were watching the parable of the burning bush. Potatoes were being carefully arranged one upon another, but the pile seemed to grow no larger, Jessie peered intently through the gloom the lads were not handing potatoes to her but Emmie still arranged them. She was slowly moving them from side to side, Then as Jessie watched, one of the lads looked round and grasped Emmie's; well where she sat down. It was positively blasphemous that Emmie should have her; where she sat down, squeezed in church, she must tell her father, he would stop it immediately, but if they stopped she would not know what may happen next.

It was so confusing to Jessie, Emmie still moved potatoes, the lad moved his hand from sight. Glad the disgusting exhibition was over, but Jessie still watched, then Emmie's dress seemed to heave and ripple in a most unusual manner, Jessie gasped, a hand fluttered to her mouth as she realised that the steady heaving of Emmie's dress was caused by a hand beneath her clothes.

Father must be told. But if father was told he would stop them at once, she would not see what would happen next. It was so confusing, no one put a hand beneath

Jessie's dress to feel her petticoats, which were of the finest material, painstakingly made by the best dressmaker in town, while Emmie's even her Sunday best were coarse and rough, plain, made with long irregular stitches. Two or three tears of self-pity rolled down her sallow cheeks onto her flat chest.

She did not know if she were glad or sorry when one of the boys picked up a handful of discarded leaves and left by the belfry door, the other soon followed. After a discreet interval, Emmie also picked up flower stalks and left. Jessie, whose instinct told her all was not over, followed out into the darkness where all was silent. Confused, heart beating rapidly she knew not why, she walked along the grass towards the back of the church, gladly, sadly, the trio had disappeared, now she would never know why the boys preferred Emmie's plain petticoats to her own finely decorated ones, or even why they wanted to feel petticoats at all.

Jessie stopped.

A slight noise had come from the shed where the sexton kept his Grave digging tools. She hurried nearer along the grass.

They were there in the shed.

Heart thumping wildly, fearful at being seen.

Fearful to find out why they were in the shed.

Now close to the shed door.

Urgent whispers from within.

"Come on Em."

"Us ownt hut yer!"

"Come on gal."

"Yer know we, if'n we gie yer a young-un one o' we ull marry yer."

Panic stricken she turned to run, her hands fluttered to cover her ears, then pick up the hem of her dress, legs weak as if rooted to the spot.

More sounds from the shed, was it a squeal of pain or laughter? Many thoughts jumbled through her head, did Emmie need help? Should you fetch her father? Or enter the shed herself? It was definitely a giggle from Emmie that time.

Desperately she wanted the boys to come out of the shed and find her, terrified one would. Her own nice untouched petticoats, it was so confusing, so disgusting so unfair.

Emmie couldn't have a baby! She wasn't married, the marriage service said marriage was to beget children.

Blindly through tears and darkness she ran, stumbling over graves, a quick crunch crunch as she crossed a gravel path, across the back lawn of the vicarage, up the back stairs to her room, she threw herself fully clothed face down onto her bed, muddy boots on the crisp white bedspread.   Tears streamed down her face as she beat her hands on the pillows, it was confusing, so unsatisfactory, so unfair.

Chapter 6
Bonfire

"Wot yew taken this year then Sid?"

"Oi dunno yit Bor."

"Yew grut owd liar, Oi see yew a-putten water on yar tatters."

"Ar so be yew did, but Oi might hay a different notion this year, if Oi git a bit o' string and hang a few carrants down from the winder, Oi reckon they'd look aright."

"Oi'll gie yew that bor yew allus could grow a good carrant."

In the darkness the two men leaned on the garden wall, occasionally a glow as short clay pipes were sucked, they listened as the sound of hob-nailed boots clomped nearer along the road.

"Woop Bertie."

"Coop Sid."

Brief greetings were exchanged as the men met.

"Sid say he agowen ter tak carrants fer his winder this year."

"How about iffen Missus Jeeves want they up the

front?"

"Oi'll chucka few tatters in me owd barrer tew."

"Iffen youm as wicked as owd Ned say Oi down know why you bovver ter goo ter chuch attall, you'm past prayyen fer."

Silence as pipes were sucked and rekindled, a cough a spit.

"Whoi wass owd Ned got aggin he?"

"Fore yore time bor, fore yew commed this way."

A hawk a spit to prolong the drama.

"Bonfire night it wor, us commed out the Free Fevvers at tunnen out toime, a bit o'fire the owd boys had still bunt, us went over an owd Ned he start ter roun ut up, make ut blaze up loike. Loike a lot o' fewels us started ter git a few sticks ter make ut up ou.

"Carn yew dew better nor that?" owd Ned hollers.

So Oi slips over his garden hedge an chucked out one of his faggots, somebody lugged ut ter owd Ned, an he brook ut open an chucked ut on ter fire.

"Thass the stuff" he holler "kip ut commen.

Oi wucked loik a gooden, chucken his faggots over his hidge, tothers they carted they ter he, Ned he chucked they on the fire, that own man had ha some beer that night, arter we'd bunt awl his faggots he still kep hollerun "kip ut commen".

Oi took his spade an broke orf his privy door, a couple o

they lugged ut ter he, soons he'd chucked ut on the fire he knew where ut ha come from, did'n he swear? Iffen awl he say come true Oi owdunt be here now. Nex day when Oi goo back ter wuk artter dinner, there he sot, in his privy wi' no door."

"Woop Ned" oi say.

He never say northun, juss sot there a smoken away on his owd pipe. Ut were a rare long while afore he got annuver door, moos days arter dinner there he sot smoken away. His owd woman used ter het ter wait till ut were dark afore she went down ter t' privy.

They owd boys doan dew northen loik we used ter dew in ter owd days, doan know they born half on en, well be yew lot gonna stan here awl night ajawen, or be yew accommen down the Free Fevvers fer a wet?"

Chapter 7
Michaelmas Christmas

At six o'clock work started in the farm buildings and cow-yard, the cow-men and girls milked the cows, milking over, the men attended to the stock while the girls worked in the dairy, skimming cream from the previous day's milk, making butter or cheese, an almost never ending pile of milk buckets, butter and cheese making equipment to wash and sterilize with boiling water.

Dolly, a small rosy cheeked girl of some fifteen summers, had been working in the dairy only a few weeks when Mr Wex entered the dairy one morning, he instructed her to go to a certain part of the woods, with a message for Ted Owls the forester to return to the farmyard at once.

Mounting his thoroughbred hunter, Mr Wex rode off in the opposite direction, then circled round to the wood where Dolly was still searching for Ted, who was working in a far distant part of the estate.

"Have you told Owls to go back to the yard yet girl?"

"No Zur, Oi carnt find he."

"You know what happens to girls who don't do as

they're told?"

"No Zur."

Mr Wex tied his horse to a tree, threw his heavy riding cloak to the ground.

"Lay down here girl I'll show you."

This routine, with slight variations continued all summer, until one morning at their daily conference, the house-keeper Mrs Towers told Mr Wex.

"We'll have to get rid of Dolly, she's with child."

"Leave it to me Mrs Towers, we'll not get rid of her yet, she's the best cheese maker we've had."

The hiring fair was held at Hotchly, the first Wednesday after michaelmas. Fair day always a local holiday, from early morning, pony-traps carts, carriages, wagons, wheelbarrows, people on foot, all laden with produce to sell, streaming into town from the surrounding villages. Stall-holders selling all kinds of goods alive or dead, new or second-hand, arriving early to via for the best pitches. The usual weekly auction market, full with produce, and overflowing into a nearby meadow.

Horses, ponies, donkeys, cattle were paraded up and down market meadow for sale privately, or by auction later in the day. Gypsy dealers in small colourful groups, always on the lookout for anyone with enough money to buy, any interest shown exploited to the full.

Men, women, parents with children seeking a hiring for

a year or longer, paraded up and down market street, advertising their trade, by carrying something of their calling, a shepherd carried his crook, a horseman a whip, a thatcher a plait of straw round his hat, not leaving the market place until hired, or the fair died down late at night.

Four wagons, full of people and produce had left Rockness Hall at day-break for the fair, each horse, it's tail and mane gaily be-ribboned, brasses burnished bright, sale goods crammed into the wagons, vegetables, eggs, carved walking sticks, a goat or two tied with string.

Everybody in their Sunday best clothes, what few pennies they had carefully hidden beneath mysterious folds in their garments. A long time spent at each stall before purchases were made, of ribbons, lace, second-hand clothes or boots, horse brasses, ale or gin from stall or inn for those with money left.

Mr Wex having driven himself into town, left his horse with the ostler at the Black Catt Inn, walked among the crowds in Market Street, he paused to talk to several men before he found one who satisfied his critical inspection, Joe Bell by name, horseman by trade, single, aged about twenty, he was hired and told to take his bundle of belongings to the Black Cat and wait for Charlie, the Hall horse keeper.

Charlie, found at the brassware stall, was given a few shillings by Mr Wex, Joe Bell was to be liberally supplied with enough ale and gin to make him completely intoxicated.

Charlie got his final order.

"But not you, I'll have no one drunk in charge of my horses."

Six o'clock, departure time, saw the horses hitched to the Rockness Hall wagons, men, women and children had gathered in the yard of the Black Cat Inn, an excited comparing of purchases, a last drink. Charlie and a carter carried the now immobile, Joe Bell from the Inn and propped him in a wagon, his bundle of belongings beside him.

There were off, shouting, singing, laughing, a half mile from town, urgent requests for a stop beside a tall hedge, a woman in the leading wagon wailing.

"Hinery, Oi aint not got Hinery, Hinery's lorst."

"Hinery, a small boy in a faded blue jersey, hand-me-down shorts that reached his ankles, was retrieved from another wagon, and returned to his snivelling mother, who was so pleased by his return that she smacked his face with great spirit. A few odd couples who wished to dally were herded back to the wagons and they continued on their way.

Through the village, up the lane, the singing grew louder to prove to those who had to stay at home, what a good time they were having.

Mr Wex and Mrs Towers, stood by the front porch watching the wagons unload, people who lived in the village, or down the lane, walked away calling loud goodnights, a group of singers the last to leave.

Joe Bell was retrieved from the wagon floor and carried, an arm each over the shoulders of two men, Mr Wex called.

"Bring him this way."

To Dolly

"He do?"

"Ay Zue he'll do."

Joe was heaved up the back stairs and dumped on Dolly's bed.

"Take his boots off girl."

Dolly was left with her future husband. The door was propped shut from the outside by a chair across the landing, and Rockness Hall settled down to sleep.

At five o'clock next morning Mr Wex stormed into the bedroom, Dolly sat up in bed naked, Joe Bell still snoring drunkenly by her side was awakened.

"What the devil do you think you're doing man? I should horsewhip you, I hire you as a horseman, not a stallion and find you in bed with one of my maids, you'll have to marry her, I'll see the parson, be at the church four o'clock Saturday."

Joe and Dolly were given the use of a cottage in the lane, Mrs Towers supplied the bare household necessities, a saucepan, a kettle, a frying pan, blankets.

Late November, Dolly gave birth to a son, the first of many, Joe celebrating at the inn was heard to boast.

"From Michaelmass to Christmas, a new wife, a new job, a new house, a new baby, it must be my lucky year."

Chapter 8
Jack the Pack

The rumour spread rapidly through the village, Jack The Pack was in the neighbourhood, a few days later he arrived at Rockness, calling at farms, houses any cottage that had anyone at home.

A short dapper man, highly polished brown boots and leggings, riding breeches, winter or summer a long black coat, a bushy snow white beard, the whole crowned by a well worn, shabby black silk top hat. The pack carried on his back a contrivance of his own design and manufacture, the pack when opened out on the ground or table, its many pockets displayed a vast amount of cheap haberdashery, boot laces, buttons, sewing cotton, needles, ribbons, lace, hat pins, brooches, small trinkets of all descriptions.

At the Hall he was invited into the kitchen by Mrs Towers, whereon, with a flourish he presented her with a gaudily decorated hat pin. Pack open on the kitchen table he started his sales patter, items in turn were picked up as he told of their virtues. The beautiful colours of the ribbons, the fine quality of the embroidery silk, the sharpness of needles, bootlaces that would hardly ever wear out.

After all had feasted their eyes on his ware, a few items purchased, the pack was refolded, the straps refastened, a piece of bread and cheese in his hand to eat as he trudged along and Jack the Pack had gone for another year.

By evening he was nearly through the village, he called at a small cottage, tell tale smoke from a chimney revealed someone was at home, he spread his pack on the path near the back door and knocked sharply, as the door opened he started his sales patter, it was minutes before the woman could get a word in.

"Oi carnt not buy nuff un, Oi aint not got no money."

"Yar husbun he'll buy yer summat pretty?"

"E gon orf wi a hoss, E ownt be back fer tew hour."

She stood on the doorstep, wiping her hands on a filthy sack apron.

"Look at they needless gal, real good an sharp they be, they brooches, sold one ter the parson's Mrs she say she agowan ter wear ut ter chuch cum Sunday.

On his knees he crept round his pack, picking things up at random from the neatly arranged pockets.

"Look at they hat pins gal, ain't they pretty, all the way from It'ly they cum, thass where all the best hat pins come from."

"Yer di'nt git they from It'ly."

"Oi do gal, Oi goo up ter Lunnon, an git they orf a ship wot comes fro' It'ly."

He now knelt by her side holding a string of highly coloured glass beads.

"Doan they lok pretty? Roun yar kneck they'd look real bootyfull."

The beads were carefully displayed on a bare patch of canvas, a button hook was produced, he demonstrated the ease with which he could unbutton her shoes, his hand be carefully forgot to remove from her ankle as he prattled on, a bunch of wax cherries he held up.

"The beat wot ever come from It'ly wot ever would they look like roun' yar bess hat ter chuch cum Sunday?"

The cherries were placed by the necklace and the buttonhook.

"Woun yew loik they gal? Yew'd loik awright wi' yhey on."

His roving hand left her in no doubt how they could be hers. A hatpin, the end a gaudy wax apple was held up, he stood up the hand under her volumous clothes caressing the small of her back.

"Cum on gal, less goo down the garden."

Gently but firmly the hand round her waist pushed her forward.

The two men walking quietly along the edge of the cornfield at the bottom of the garden, would have passed by but for their dogs. The dogs had stopped, tails stretched rigid out behind them, their muzzles pointed towards the garden, sharp ears picked out unidentified rustling in the garden.

One at a time the poachers crawled silently far enough into the garden hedge to see the couple in the grass.

The men made no sound as they continued on their way. A mile further on they heard the sound of a cart horse plodding along, when near enough to be sure who it was they stepped into the roadway, the three brothers stopped to talk, a pheasant was passed up into the cart, it would be a very foolhardy gamekeeper who would wish to search the squires own cart.

Silas, one of the brothers on foot was the first to speak.

"Us be gowan up ter 'Roun' Wood ternite ter see Jack T' Pack."

"Whoi?"

"It worn't yew a layen under yar curran bushes ou yar Missues, an she ou har skut roun har kneck."

"Oi'll be ready about harf ten."

"Ah harf ten he'll be abed."

Back in his cottage, horse and cart delivered back to the stables, Jonas sat at the table, his wife gave him his meal, boiled potatoes and stewed rabbit.

Halfway through his meal before he spoke,

"Jack the Pack call today?"

"Oi gie he a penny fer a hat pin?"

"That wornt all he got."

"Oi never did."

"Silas and Horus see yer froo the hidge layed along a he unner the curran bush Oi out no cloes."

"Doan hit Oi Jonas."

"Oi gowan ter gie yer a black eye when Oi finish eaten."

"Doan hit Oi Jonas, yew know Oi can help ut when Oi'm on song."

"Oi gowan ter gie yer a black eye then see if youm still on song."

Four of the five brothers met at half past ten, they liked to be called Us Brothers, Thomas, Silas, Jonus and Horace. All were used to moving silently at night about the countryside. Dogs by their side they approached Round Wood where the packman was encamped, the usual camping place for travellers who could not afford the few pence needed to lodge at the inn or lodging house.

Two approached from either side, the camp fire nearly out, Jack asleep under a piece of canvas supported by sticks. A heavy blow from a cudgel, waking him at the same time almost stunning him.

"Wos a marrer ou yew lot?"

"Us reckon yew gi too much ter his Missus."

"Oi never."

"Yew did an' yew a gowan ter pay."

Heavy sticks struck him from all sides as he scrambled to his feet, the dogs stood in a circle snarling, if signalled by an owner each would willing have joined in the affray. The packman could stand no longer and collapsed on top of this tent. A heavy boot kicked his crotch, each man gave a vicious kick in the same area, they left him unconscious on the ground.

"That'll larn he, he ownt not worry nobody's Missus fer a day err two."

Chapter 9
May

Everyone was aware that May the parlour-maid had broken a vase, on the spot she had been given a couple of blows on the shoulders with a broom, the housekeeper had then given her the option of in the house punishment or "to go to look at the crossroads", which meant instant dismissal and to be dumped bag and baggage at the crossroads outside the village. From the crossroads the chance of a job in a decent household very remote, no possibility of return to the village, all the dwellings belonging to church or the Hall, any one found harbouring a refugee even close family liable to instant eviction.

May had chosen to stay at Rockness. Sunday after the midday meal had been chosen as a suitable time for the chastising ceremony. The meal cleared away and washing up finished, the household staff packed the kitchen. Orders from Mr Wex were that females were not to be naked when punishment was being given. May entered, having been instructed by Mrs Towers to wear boots and best black dress, nothing else, leaning forward, fore-arms on the seat of a kitchen chair, the dress had been pulled upwards, only the collar under her chin prevented it from being pulled completely off.

Mrs Towers wielded the heavy leather strap like a professional, the leather fairly whistled through the air and landed on May's shoulders, each successive stroke lower until the last of the ten awarded was delivered sideways to the top of her legs. May's back now a mass of angry red weals, her instructions on how to handle delicate china were over.

Sue the youngest of the maids was allowed to help and support May as she staggered to her feet and up the back stairs to her attic room.

The boys and girls whose afternoon off it was, were now allowed to leave the kitchen. The other girls who had no specific duty, sat on the hard wooden chairs and took up their embroidery, making or mending clothes on Sunday was not permitted, making anything useful was a sin, so the girls sat hour after hour, decorating handkerchiefs, or making samplers.

The boys although not restricted to the house were not permitted to leave the farm.

Chapter 10
Rev Holly

Six pairs of horses slowly neared the end of the field, they stopped in a line abreast. Two of the ploughmen hurried of, each took from his plough a short narrow spade, used for cleaning his plough, but now to be used for an entirely illegal purpose. The two men were the most skilful at catching rabbits and quickly disappeared into a nearby spinney, while the other four men attended their horses, confident that any game caught would be shared fairly.

A nosebag containing a mixture of ground oats and chaff was strapped to each horses head, the men took overcoats and dinner bags and sat in a row by the roadside hedge.

Conversation at meal times sparse, even the weather only mentioned if it directly concerned their work.

Dan the last to sit down, the others already eating.

"Lew bor, aint yew got northun ter put yar fum on?"

Lew sat, large chunk of bread in one hand, open knife in the other.

"Shant hay no fummer, not while cum payday."

Dan sat, opened his wickerwork dinner basket, his meal consisted of the bottom half of a cottage loaf and a hunk of cheese, the cheese he neatly halved, one piece he dropped onto Lews open kerchief.

"Yew carn wuk on bread alone Bor."

Dan dropped his bread and cheese onto the grass, two fingers of each hand in his mouth he blew a sharp double whistle of alarm, then continued eating as if nothing had happened.

The twelve horses lifted their heads in surprise, twenty-four ears swivelled to pinpoint the danger signal, satisfied the danger did not concern them they continued to munch their oats and chaff.

Dan and his three companions sat unconcernedly eating, one spoke, voice indistinct through a mouthful of bread and cheese.

"Dew he would come along juzs now."

The vehicle approached to within a few yards and stopped, the four men stood and respectfully with thumb and forefinger, each pinched the peak of his cap, a mumbled chorus of,

"Morning reverend."

"Morning Sims, Wright, Andrews, Bones, I see two of your number are missing, up to no good I presume?"

"No Zur they awright."

One of the missing ploughmen emerged from the

spinney dragging a long stick, the cut end as thick round as his thumb, as he walked he cut off the leafy twigs and threw them into the hedge.

"Morning reverend Holly."

As he spoke he tweaked the peak of his cap.

"Oive hay moi eye on this here bit o hazel fer a rare long while, now uts juss roit fer a bow fer me owd sythe. Do Oi leave ut they owd day min ull thieve ut, take anything they would."

The other missing ploughman appeared, making an unnecessary rustling as he forced his way through the hedge, as if highly embarrassed he made a pantomime of touching the peak of his cap, holding up his corduroy trousers and groping under his jacket and garnsey for his braces.

"Beg pardon Reverend, had ter goo, sony toime us git."

The Reverend Holly sat on his tricycle and distastefully eyed them up and down over the top of his gold rimmed spectacles and under the foreward tilted brim of his hard black ecclesiastical hat.

"You're an untrustworthy lot, I shall most certainly inform your employer that you wandered away leaving your horses untended, I bid you Good-day."

The peaks of six caps were again respectfully pinched.

The Reverend Holly backed his pedals until the left was in the high position, then simultaneously pushing with his left foot, with his right he kicked the rump of his dog, urging it forward with a sharply spoken.

"Pull away you lazy hound."

When out of earshot the usual argument started among the ploughmen.

"That owd bugger he lorst Oi a rabbit, O'id nearly got ut out of a hole on a bit o bramble when yew lot a whistled, iffen Oi slip orf agin Oi'll be back afore yew tun the hosses roun."

Resh and Willie hurried back to the spinney, while the other four men returned to the horses to prepare for the afternoon's work. All six ploughs were turned to face the field when the poachers returned, with gee ups and tongues clicking, the twelve horses and six men set of across the field. At the far end of the field Resh walked casually along behind the row of ploughs which the men were cleaning, without pausing beside three of the ploughs he dropped a rabbit, which was scooped up and promptly hidden amongst the recipient's garments.

As they started back across the field, from the same poachers pocket inside his jacket, he took his bread and cheese which he ate as he walked a swig of cold tea completed his meal.

The argument continued all afternoon, Resh and Willie apposed the actions of the Reverend Holly, Lew and Ben agreed with the parson, the other two supporting either side when the argument seemed to be slacking.

Resh declared.

"Taint roit a dawg is fer ter ketch rabbits not ter pull he on his owd trike."

This brought from Lew.

"He ony kick that there owd dowg when he start up, or on t ter hills."

From somewhere along the row of men.

"How sum ever, if a dawg wore meant ter pull he ut ort ter hay a proper harness."

A sulky silence as the men ploughed from one end of the field and back, chains were unhooked, reins were coiled up, the argument finally decided by Ben.

"He's a parson, do ut were wrong he'd a read about ut in t' boible."

Chapter 11
Bath Night

It was a wet and steamy business, steam rose from the two copper boilers, the fires of which the kitchen boy kept well stoked with wood, as he was last in line it was also to his benefit to have hot water to the end. The girls, naked, clothes draped shawl ways over shoulders waited in the kitchen to come forward in order of age to take their turn in the water.

The bath in the centre of the wash house, the bottom half of a large barrel, clothes when taken off dropped into another barrel to await Monday's wash.

Mrs Towers always supervised from her chair, as if ruling from a throne, if the washing not energetic enough for her pleasure, a floor scrubbing brush in hand to assist, to scrub vigorously where she considered not enough attention being made. Face, hair, body, male or female parts, all scrubbed with strong carbolic soap. When the victim was clean enough, Mrs Towers shouted out, the clean body stood up, the kitchen boy poured a pail of hot water over the head to rinse away soap suds, step onto a board to dry with a rough towel the next in line naked ready to step into the tub.

The boys waited their turn in an adjacent outhouse, peep-holes had long ago been bored in the wooden dividing wall, eyes glued to watch the proceedings, all were aware of this, some of the girls while standing to lather turning to give the watchers a more tantalising view.

The boys in the darkness watched with bated breath, the girl in the tub, Winnie, a shapely lass of some seventeen summers, stood up to lather her body, appreciative whispers led to a statement by Jack Always.

"Oi'll see she loik that arter chuch come Sunday."

"Yew leave she alone, she a'moi."

"Oi'll see she if'n Oi loik George Cox, she doan belong a yew."

"Oi see she fust."

"No yew did'n."

"Oi didn'awl when we had ter move that there funitur."

"No yew didn."

"Yew come inter t orchun an Oi'll show yew."

"Oi'll hit yew on ter snout."

"Come on dew yew reckon yew can."

Out in the quiet darkness of the orchard, a short sparring around a glancing blow landed on a chest, the contestants grappled and shuffled about arms locked around each other.

"Us be missen the rest o' they!"

The dead-lock was over, differences forgotten, George and Jack hurried back to try to regain their place at the peep holes.

Chapter 12
Jeany

Jeany wife of one of the carter's, again pregnant, she had not asked Charlie but one day, while working in the field announced.

"Oi'll git Charlie ter calve Oi down this toime, he calved Anna awright, Oi doan wan that dutty owd Ginny agin."

Jeany, her baby now heavy within her, left their cottage as soon as it became dark, she had cleared away after their sparce meal of boiled potatoes and the watered down gravy of Sunday's rabbit.

She moved silently to the back door of Charlie's cottage, at her knock the door was opened a few inches until Charlie could see who his visitor was, no one moved after dark unless of sheer necessity, poachers and smugglers ready to inflict serious injury on innocent witnesses to insure the need to keep quiet of their identity or whereabouts.

As she entered he put out the paraffin lamp that had been burning on the kitchen table, Jeany, he knew had come to discuss terms, they sat on wooden chairs by the fire in the kitchen range, got up filled his pipe from a tin on the mantle-shelf, lit up and sat down again at last Jeany spoke.

"How much dew yew wan ter calve oi down Charlie?"

Charlie smoked on in silence.

"Oi gie Ginny a shillun afore."

Another long companiable silence, the fire was stoked up, the clay pipe refilled.

"Oi'll gie yer anuvver thru pence on top!"

After another long silence, Charlie passed Jeany the refilled and steadily burning pipe and entered the discussion.

"Oi niver said Oi wanted money orfa yew gal, yew aint not got none ter spare."

Jeany puffed on, blowing clouds of black smoke up the chimney.

"Wot dew tew want?"

A longer silence as this critical question was considered.

"Yew."

Another long silence, the empty pipe was passed back.

"Yarl look arter Oi."

A question and a statement, his answer.

They sat in silence until Charlie deemed it time for the interview to end, he stood and standing behind Jeany's chair, undone the buttons at the back of her dress, she leaned her head back to give him room to manoeuvre, his hand under several layers of petticoats he groped around.

"Yar udders be awright gal!"

He refastened the buttons, she stood up he sat in the chair she had just vacated, his hand under her long black dress. Jeany straddled her legs wide apart, an involuntary wince as rough fingers snagged on delicate membranes, her prenatal inspection was over.

"Yew can hev Oi now Charlie."

"No gal, wouldn't be right, wouldn't be right till yew calve, Oi doan git paid till Oi dew me wuk,"

Rhueben sat smoking more of his foul black shag tobacco as she re-entered her home, without looking up.

"Yew see Charlie?"

"Ah, he say he'll calve Oi down if fun Oi gie he a shillun."

Jeany left her work in the root field at mid-day meal time, her only explanation to the other workers.

"Oi a gowan hoom."

Frantically busy all afternoon, she swept the bedroom, washing the brick floor of the kitchen and floor and seat of the earth closet at the far end of the garden and boiled potatoes for Rhuebens' tea, soon after she had washed the saucepan, two plates and two forks.

"Rhueben, goo git Charlie?"

"Rhueben knocked on Charlie's door, it was opened the usual three inches."

"She say ull yew cum along Bor?"

From the dark interior of the kitchen Charlie replied.

"Goo back Bor, tell she Oi'll be along."

The door closed, Charlie took a long swig from a bottle of home-brewed wine, he had a long coughing spasm as the strong drink took his breath away, another swig, the oil lamp turned out, down the back garden path, along the field to Rhueben's garden, where he pushed through the hedge and up to the back door.

He let himself in, Rhueben sat by the fire, cap still on head, sucking an empty pipe, Jeany stood leaning heavily forward, both arms on the table. Sitting on the single vacant chair, Charlie took off his boots and placed them under the table.

Jeany paced back and forth, wall to wall, then rested leaning on the table, Rhueben passed Charlie his tobacco tin, no sound, only the creak of the table as Jeany rested her weight on it.

"We'll goo up when yar ready gal."

"Not yit Charlie, not yit."

Back and forth she shuffled, back and forth, another rest, a sharp intake of breath, she turned and leaned on the door that opened to the stairs. Charlie took off his jacket, hung it on a nail and helped her up the narrow stairs, a long and awkward progress on all fours, a step up, the long dress and apron to pull up, a slow crawl across the landing into the bedroom, Charlie put down on a chest of drawers the candle that he carried and helped her to her feet.

"Yew ownt make Oi lay on that bloody bed till Oi hetta, will yew Charlie?"

She pleaded.

"Ginny ouldn't let Oi move."

She clung to him, head on his shoulder.

"Yarl dew nigh enough what yew wantew Gal, ony yew an Oi'll know what happens up here this night."

"Let Oi walk agin.

Hanging on to each other they shuffled across the small room, backwards and forwards, wall to wall, a rest then on again, she stopped, tried to undo the buttons at the back of her dress.

"Help Oi Charlie."

The sack apron was thrown into a corner, the dress followed, then one after another her petticoats followed.

Naked she continued her restless movement, clinging more tightly to Charlie as her labour pains grew closer and closer. Her face and body now covered with sweat, he had great difficulty in controlling her awkward weight.

"Let Oi down Charlie, he's cumin."

Jeany knelt, forearms on the floor, head on her arms, almost immediately the baby stared to appear, a black head of hair.

Charlie kept up a continual stream of encouragement.

"Yewm awright Gal, let he come when he wantew help he when he wanner come, doan hurry he, he'm awright."

He took the weight of the baby's head in his hands.

"Your aright Gal, help he ter come when he wanner come, he'm aright."

With a rush the baby was born into his strong careful hands, he cleaned it's face with a wet rag, it's mouth and nose, it sneezed a couple of times waved it's pudgy arms and breathed, he wrapped it in a towel and placed it on the bed.

"Come on Gal, bed now."

He lifted her up and placed her on the bed beside her son, with warm water from a pail, he washed her face and body, covered her up and cleaned up the room.

"Oi'll tell Rueben he can come up now Gal."

"No not yit Charlie, let Oi sleep fust."

Chapter 13
Storm

Rockness Hall stands on high ground, to the East woods separated it from the headland and the North sea, South and West, lush pastures and rich fields, to the North the woods dropped to a small tidal creek, the far side of which stands Foulrock Farm, part of the Rockness estate, the farmhouse long ago destroyed by fire. Reached only at low tide by a ford across the steam, Foulrock Farm had many acres of marshy land, lush grazing in this summer, flooded regularly in the winter. The farm buildings were still standing on a few acres of high ground, consisted of a stout stone walled square that housed barns and stockyards and a row of stone built cottages, only one of which was now in use. The occupants were Ted and Anna, Ted looked after the cattle, during this summer they grazed the marshes, in the winter the yards were full, Ted fed and watered them. Charlie driving his horse and cart over each day to supervise.

The storm blowing in from the East had raged all day

Charlie had crossed the creek at low tide, his cart laden with cattle feed and a few household necessities that Anna needed, even at low tide the water had reached the horses belly, the hard track through the creek marked by painted posts would be impassable if the wind kept up.

All day Charlie and Ted worked in the cattle yards, giving them food, water and clean bedding straw. The huge barn doors were securely tied shut with wagon ropes, as a precaution against the high wind, one door failing, the whole structure would have been at risk.

As the time for low tide approached, the men made frequent trips to check the level of water in the creek, the wind was driving the sea water into the creek, no attempt could be made to cross that day.

Anna, now pregnant and near her time had worked about the cottage and their own animals all day, cooked a midday meal of vegetables and grilled fish over the fire in the kitchen range.

After their tea, hurricane lamps were lit, the two men walked through the lashing rain to the cattle yards, checking all was well and the storm doing no harm. By common consent a trip was made to the crossing to watch the great foaming waves crash into the bay. On their return to the warm kitchen Anna announced her intention of going to bed, they could hear the floorboards creak as she walked about the upstairs room. An hour or more later she called from the top of the stairs.

"Ted, Ted."

He reluctantly opened the door to the stairs.

"Ted yarl hetta git Ginny."

Ginny was the self appointed midwife, her nickname came from her partiality to gin. Short, dumpy, a wizened little face, she would lay out the dead and if necessary go direct to a birth, pausing only to spend any money earned on gin. Always smelling of stale sour alcohol and unwashed body, to her, if it ever crossed her mind, washing and clean clothes an unnecessary waste of time.

Stomping along in her hob nailed boots, she was a familiar figure in the village and surrounding district, a cloth bag swinging from her hand containing not medical necessities, but a bottle of gin.

The longer a birth took, the more gin she drank, the more she drank the more bad tempered she became, the temper brought impatience, swearing and violence causing unnecessary pain and often irreparable damage to mother and child.

The men looked to each other for support, putting on boots and overcoats, each man a stick and lanthorn, they tried to hurry against the driving wind to the crossing, huge waves driving ashore covered even the crossing marker posts, no help could arrive that night.

Back in the kitchen all seemed quiet as the men hung up their wet overcoats to dry, but as they stood they could hear Anna crying, a sharp squeal of pain then crying again.;

"What the hell can Oi do Bor?"

Ted fetched a bottle of homemade wine and a couple of mugs.

Morning and the men after a long night of hearing Anna alone in her distress, again went to the crossing, waves still smashing into the creek dashed away any forlorn hope they may have had.

One at a time they left the cottage to attend the cattle.

After a morning of drinking and worrying, Ted at last.

"Charlie yarl hetta calve she down!"

Charlie sat drinking more and more of the potent wine.

Over and over again Ted repeated.

"Charlie, yarl hetta calve she down."

At last Charlie was goaded to snarl in reply.

"Yew bloody ol' fewl, Oi aint niver sin a woman calve, nor yit helped."

"No Bor, but yewm a bloody good stockman, yew doan lose cow nor calf; woman, cow, sorl the same."

Darkness, the noise of the wind and rain, partly drowning the sounds from upstairs, now an intermittent moaning, Ted at last forced himself upstairs to look at his wife, slumping back into a chair at the table.

"Charlie, we'll lose she ifn yew doan calve she soon!"

Standing with difficulty, a bottle of wine in one hand, a candle in the other, Charlie lurched to the stairs, in the bedroom after intense concentration managed to set both candle and bottle safely on a chest of drawers, turned to the bad where Anny lay exhausted.

"Wasser marrer ou yew gal?"

He pulled away the blankets that covered her.

"Ifn yew wore a cow Oid soon ha that there calf out."

Hiccuping loudly he called down the stairs.

"Giss that there hot water!"

"The door opened a grey-face Ted handed in a wooden bucket containing hot water, Charlie made a soapy lather on his hands."

"Oi hope yew can stand ut owd gal."

He gently pushed his fingers into her, his hand inside he muttered to himself.

"Yewm got the little bugger side 'uds on."

Instead of a head he could feel the baby's back.

"Dew yew kip still, dew yew can Gal."

Alcoholic sweat poured down his face, he tried to push the baby back to turn it, each time he seemed to be succeeding a spasm shook her body and again the baby moved down back first.

Blinded by sweat he worked harder, his fingers felt a tiny shoulder, his thumb a neck, the other shoulder, another push, the baby turned towards him, his fingers guiding it's head down, it followed his hand down.

"Let he come now Gal, when yew loik, oi'll help he."

He wiped his face on his shirt sleeve, he could see the dark hair on it's head, now it's forehead, she paused to retain strength, a final groan, with a rush the baby was born.

With a wet towel he wiped the child's face, its nose and mouth, it sneezed and was breathing, from his jacket pocket he took a piece of sting, his shut knife from his trousers pocket, he tied the umbilical cord, he trimmed off the string and cut the cord.

Carefully he wrapped the infant in a towel and placed it by the mother's side, he could not pull her night-dress up high enough or down far enough for the baby to suckle, so again using the shut knife, he put two fingers in the collar and slit the gown down to the waist, the baby began to suckle immediately.

Downstairs Ted sat by the table, head in his hands, Charlie, elated at the success of the birth, kicked the table leg with his heavy boot, clapped both hands on Ted's back.

"Yew young fewel yew, yar woman an yar colt 're gowan ter be aright."

The storm raged for two more days before it broke,

three before Charlie could return home over the creek and spread the good news.

Spring turned to summer, glorious hot summer days, Ted now worked in the harvest fields, Charlie daily visited the cattle that grazed on the marshes, a cart now not needed for cattle feed, rode the study bay cob the length and breadth of the marshes, checking each animal under his care.

His round of inspection completed for the day, he let the pony pick its own way back to the farm, the reins loose on the animals' neck as he cut thin slivers from a plug of black shag tobacco, rubbed it carefully between rough hands, filled and lit his pipe. Cap pulled over his eyes, he sat motionless as the pony ambled gently along, the bowl at his broken stemmed clay pipe under his nose, as the rank smoke drifted up his nostrils, only an occasional puff proved him not to be asleep. Along the shingle beach to the rocky out-crop from which the farm got it's name, up the cliff path, through the woods, out to the pasture near the farm,

The pony he put into one of the empty cattle pens, plenty of time to see Anna and the baby before the tide turned and water covered the causeway. The farmstead was quiet and empty, even the hens had succumbed to the heat and were asleep in the shade, no smoke from a cooking fire in the cottage chimney, he knew where he could find Anna on a day such as this. Most days she spent in the cove, setting long lines of fish hooks along the mud flats on the incoming tide. If not fishing she would be beachcombing, the cove always yielding something useful.

Long ago Anna, being unable to wait for the recedeing tide to uncover her lines, had waded into the sea to retrieve fish from her hooks, splashing from marker post to marker post, at home her thick woollen dress had been heavy and cold, difficult to dry. The next day, aware she was always alone in the isolated cove, had taken off all her clothes. This was now her normal practice, weather permitting, to work naked, either in the walled garden, or on the beach.

Now as soon as the baby was in his box like cradle above high tide mark, she would strip and set to work. Drift wood she carried to the top of the cliff path, reusable timber Ted would sell or barter in the village, many an outside privy, a rabbit, or ferret hutch made from wood Anna had salvaged.

Charlie followed the cliff path across the meadow to the cliff top, where were stacked timber in neat piles according to size, a huge pile of firewood, some rope Anna had found the same day.

At the far end of the beach Anna was searching among

the rocks, slowly Charlie made his way down the steep cliff path and sat by the baby, Anna never out of sight of the cradle, had seen Charlie arrive and approached without embarrassment, dropping her load of wood she lifted the child from his box and sat on the sand, before putting it to suckle she spat on each nipple and rubbed them with a petticoat to remove the sea salt.

Baby satisfied she placed it on a piece of sail cloth to kick naked in the sunshine, only then did they talk to each other.

"Charlie bor, Ted say Oi gotta ask yew summut."

Charlie grunted in rely.

"Ted say when can he roid Oi agin?"

Charlie got up walked round the cot shelter and sat down with her, gazing with approval at her salt covered body.

"Yew look aright gal, we'd best make sure."

He undressed and lay down with her, before dressing to leave.

"Youm awright gal, Oi'll hetta try yew every day ter make sure, us mayn 't hay yew agowan wrong."

Chapter 14
Fox Hunt

Traditionally the fox hounds met twice a year at Rockness Hall, once in the autumn, cub-hunting, they met early in the day, their objective to break up the litters of cubs, to leave them more evenly spread about the area, today the meet was at eleven o'clock, giving horses that had travelled far time to rest and feed. The household staff had risen early fires to light, vast quantities of food to prepare and cook, house guests to wait on and dress for the hunt. Grooms had been working hard from early hours to groom horses for Mr Wex and spare mounts for the hunt servants. The house guests with horses but no groom expected their mounts to be turned out to perfection.

The estate horsemen were on hand to hold horses while the gentry dismounted to partake of refreshment. Carriages arriving bringing those whose grooms were hacking the horses to the meet. Housemaids bringing out trays for those who were comfortably settled and did not wish to dismount. Only liveried grooms were allowed to assist the ladies to mount their horses and arrange their dresses and cloaks.

The Master of Fox-hounds raised his riding crop, a hunt servant tootled a merry little tune on his hunting horn, a few old hounds recognising the call lifted their muzzles and howled, the young ones joined in the chorus. High spirited horses champed at their mouth bits and danced in anticipation of a gallop.

The household staff not already outside serving drinks and snacks crowded doors and windows to watch the hunt move off, with the exception of Jam; not for Jam the thrill of the chase, or bawdy scraps with guard dogs, not for Jam ears torn while baiting badgers, his was a world of ankles and long woollen skirts, his time divided between sitting under the kitchen table, surrounded by bare feet and coarse working boots, or trotting to nowhere in his wheel.

Jam was the kitchen dog, to him fell the monotonous job of trotting in his wheel to turn the roasting spit in front of the kitchen fire. The meat to be roasted, huge barons of beef, a sucking pig, or a trio of roasting chickens impaled on an iron spit, to roast as Jam's wheel slowly turned the spit. If Jam stopped to rest, his alert little head resting on a spoke of the wheel, sharp beady eyes watching for titbits surreptitiously thrown to him, as he stopped Mrs Towers would give a double rap on the table with the heel of her kitchen knife and call.

"Move or off come your sweet-breads."

Where upon as if understanding this dire threat, Jam trotted on. The same threat was used to Joey. Joey the kitchen boy, standing for hours at a time, in front of the huge, black leaded kitchen cooking range basting the meat slowly turning on the spit, continually pouring ladle full of gravy over fowl or joint, the overflow caught in a pan below. A rich aroma arising with each ladle-full of the boiling sauce, the sauce a speciality of Mrs Towers, rich in herbs and spices, of apples and onions, of sparks and charcoal, of sweat and hair from the continually over-heated Joey, all combined to make a rich, thick succulent crust. If Joey paused or lingered away from his basting he too heard the double rap on the table and

"Move or off come your sweet-breads!"

The Master resplendent in pink and tall silk hat, he pointed his riding crop ahead and screamed "forrad", and led the hounds from the lawns, followed by the hunt members in order of social standing horses hooves clattering on the roadway, short toots on the hunting horn keeping the hounds under control.

A look out on a nearby hillock had seen the crop waved, he too raised an arm, a gamekeeper in a nearby thicket also saw the signal and pushed his way beneath a thick bush, he picked up and shook a wooden crate, the large dog fox inside, scrambled to regain his footing, his paws scrabbling on the powdered glass covering the floor, thereby releasing to greater effect his scent. Great was the surprise and satisfaction of the hunt to find a worthy quarry so soon.

After a hard and exciting day the hounds had been left in the care of a kennel groom to walk back to the kennels, the hunters gone their various ways, except for a chosen few who were to return to the hall for a meal. Huge joints of beef, of mutton, fowls, pies rich in fruit and meat, corks drawn from many a bottle, tales of their daring and skill told again and again. At long last, able to eat or drink no more, the guests called for their carriages, long and noisy farewells were called, leaving just the squire of Rockness Hall and his particular friend the vicar of Rockness Parish.

The housekeeper was ordered to have served in the study coffee and brandy. A huge fire of well seasoned ash logs glowed in the open hearth paraffin lamps had been lit, the men sat in comfortable well-worn leather covered arm chairs, spurs removed, knee length boots settled on footstools.

Again they relived the hunt, who had ridden well, who had fallen where, which was the better horses, the quality of the seasons foxes, until Mr Wex suggested a night-cap.

A bell rope dangling on the chimney breast was viciously jerked, Ruby, a trim sixteen year old parlour maid brought in two pewter mugs containing ale, placing a poker in the fire, she withdrew it when red hot and dipped it in the ale which she handed to the vicar, she repeated the process for the squire, picked up the tray end turned to leave but was gestured to stay by her employer.

"It's a fine piece of needlework your maid is wearing Squire Wex!"

"I'll tell you what we'll do Parson North, we'll play the cards for it."

A pack of cards were produced, a small table pulled between the chairs, amid much laughter and thumping the cards on the table, the game progressed, until at last the vicar cried.

"There you are Sir, I beat you fair and square, I knew I could win, and I claim my prize!"

Mr Wex waved a hand at Ruby.

"Turn round girl and let the vicar have the apron."

The carefully pressed and tied bows were snatched undone the trophy waved aloft.

The vicar challenged the squire.

"Now how about playing for that fine black dress?"

The cards were dealt, the vicar lost.

"I'm a fair man parson North, I'll give you another

chance."

This time the parson won, Ruby was made to turn her back to the parson while he unfastened the many small black buttons down her dress, finally retrieved it was thrown over the back of the chair with the apron. In due course each of her petticoats followed leaving her wearing only long black stockings and shoes.

"A stocking lets play for a stocking!"

"No two stockings and two shoes."

At the end of the game the two men fought to remove Ruby's shoes and stockings, at last the trophies were waved aloft, leaving her standing naked in front of the fire.

"I've nothing left to play for parson North! It will have to be for the girl."

The last game was very quiet, each man carefully playing his cards, Mr Wex stood up.

"You've won her fair and square parson North. I bid you goodnight."

He left closing the door behind him,

"Come here girl and help me off with my boots."

"But sir I'm to be married next week!"

"Well look on this as a holy introduction to marriage."

She turned from him and took his riding boot between her thighs, he placed his other boot on her naked bottom and pushed, leaving the imprint of his boot on her flesh, the other boot and his clothes were soon removed.

"On the floor girl."

Ruby could do no other than obey his demands, kneeling between her legs, he took his weight on his arms.

"Rise to me girl."

She was not quick to comply with his demand, he raised his right hand and struck her a smashing blow on her ribs.

"Up girl, up, lift yourself up."

He viciously thrust into her.

"Now work girl, that's what you're made that way for."

"Ruby started to work."

Another savage blow to the ribs.

"Not so fast you damned slut, you've no discipline, you need my riding crop across your shoulders a few times."

At last, lust sated, he dressed and pulled the bell rope, the door opened.

"My horse at once, damn you."

He left Ruby gently sobbing on the floor.

Closing the door on his guest, the squire made his unsteady way up the back stairs towards the servants quarters, another flight of stairs to the attic bedrooms he opened a door, the small room contained a narrow bed, a chest of drawers with a cracked mirror above, a chair on which neatly folded were the occupants' workday clothes.

He pulled the blankets from the sleeping girl, a light smack woke her in the flickering light of the candle he carried, she saw it was her master, tumbling out of bed she grabbed at her clothes and succeeded in finding a stocking, the stocking would be left in the squires bed as proof of where she spent the night, if it was discovered that she was absent from her room at night and no evidence left of her whereabouts it would be assumed that she was in the boy's rooms over the outhouses, the penalty, to be taken immediately, "to look at the crossroads".

The sound of the wildly galloping horse, that carried the drunken parson faded in the distance, Rockness Hall was asleep.

Lightning Source UK Ltd.
Milton Keynes UK
06 June 2010
155194UK00001B/9/P